KU-683-708

Stowaway

Sean Callery and George Brunton

Evans

Contents

A smooth take-off

"I dare you to get on and have
a look, Mikel," said Franz.
I couldn't resist, and crept up a ladder.
When I went to wave out of the window
I was amazed: we were flying!

6.

Airships like the *Hindenburg* were fast and comfortable. The take-off was so smooth people didn't even realise they had left the ground unless they were looking out.

Rising gas

I found a set of spare uniforms and put one on. When I went to the lounge someone gave me a tray of nuts and told me to walk round with it. Now I was Mikel the waiter!

A lady who smelt of nice perfume put down her champagne to take a snack, saying, "I can't believe we are being kept in the air by gas!"

There are gases all around us, including the air we breathe. Perfume is put on the skin as a liquid. As it warms and evaporates, it travels through the air as a gas.

Some gases are lighter than air so they rise. For example, party balloons that push upwards are filled with helium. The bubbles in fizzy drinks like champagne or cola are the gas carbon dioxide.

Helium or hydrogen?

I froze when the Captain came in, but he just took a peanut from my tray.

"Is the gas helium?" asked the lady.

"No, we couldn't get it so we use hydrogen," he replied.

"Is it as good?"

"Better. It's even lighter than helium so we can take ten more passengers," he replied, but I noticed he had his fingers crossed.

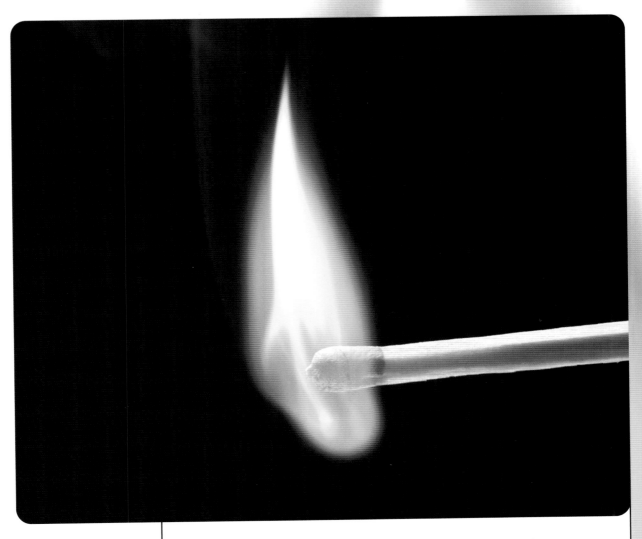

Hydrogen provides more lift than helium but it has a big drawback: it is highly flammable. That means it burns easily, unlike helium.

The airship age

The Captain pointed to the map on the wall to show how far we had already gone.
"It should take three days to get to America," he said. "That's twice as fast as by ship. Aircraft are quicker, but much more dangerous. This is the age of the airship!"

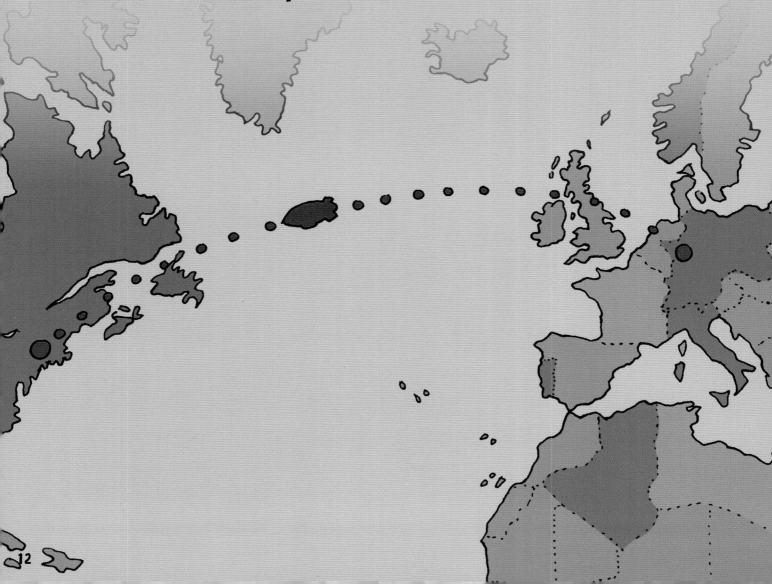

TRANSATLANTIC TRAVEL FROM EUROPE TO AMERICA IN 1937

	Journey time	Cost per ticket	Advantages	Disadvantages
Airship	3 days	$400	Luxurious and stylish. Very smooth journey – no airsickness. Safe	Expensive. Can't fly in bad weather.
Plane	29 hours	$375	Fast	Uncomfortable. Airsickness. Can't fly in really bad weather. Dangerous. Can't take many passengers.
Cruise ship	6 days or more	About $200 – much more for a bigger cabin.	Can take many passengers. Hotel-like comfort for those who can afford it. Can sail in most weathers	Slow, so journey takes a long time. Seasickness.

Metal frame

I found a long metal walkway along the middle of the ship. I could see how it was made.

The *Hindenburg* was a type of rigid airship called a dirigible: a massive metal frame covered with cloth.

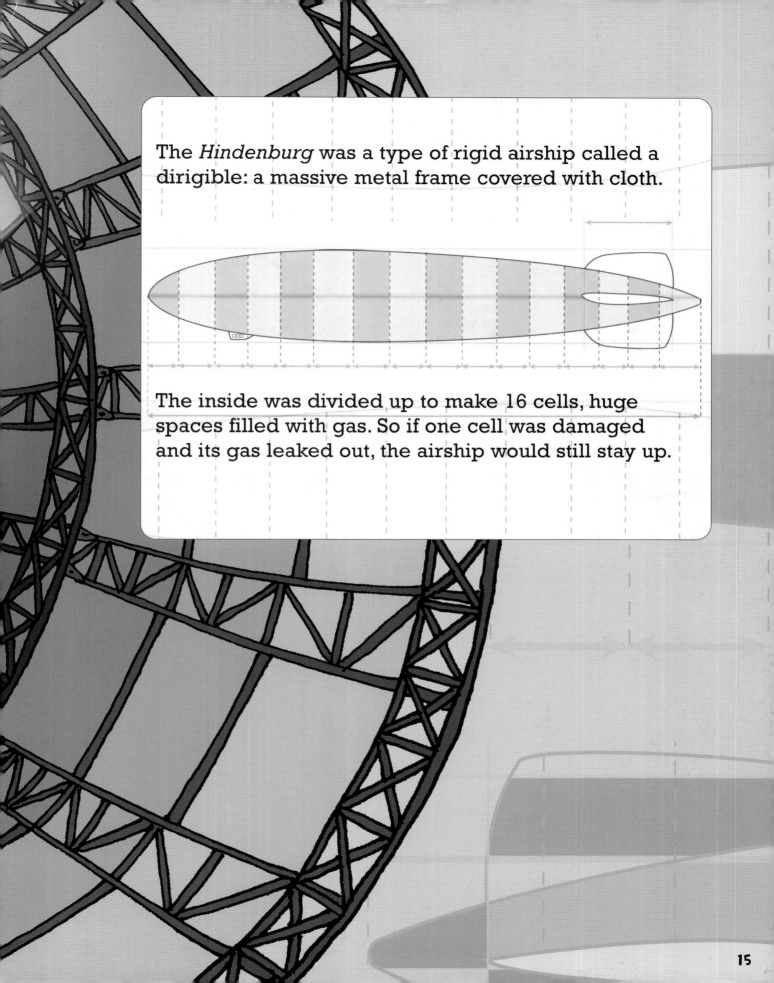

The inside was divided up to make 16 cells, huge spaces filled with gas. So if one cell was damaged and its gas leaked out, the airship would still stay up.

Luxury!

I slept in a spare cabin and dreamed I heard music. When I woke up I found it was real. I went to the lounge where the perfumed lady was singing beside a grand piano.

There were 36 passengers on board, although there was room for 70. They spent most of their time in the larger public rooms like the lounge and dining area. There was even a smoking room, sealed off to make sure no sparks reached the gas cells.

Powerful engines

The perfumed lady stopped singing and I listened to the drone of the engines.

We would arrive in New Jersey, in America, very soon.

The *Hindenburg* was powered by four 1,200 horsepower diesel engines. They provided a top speed of 135km/h (84mph) and could work in reverse to help the airship land, when the wind blew the airship about.

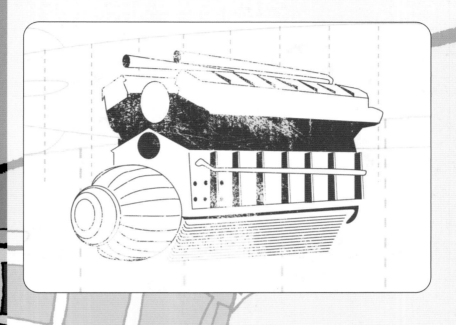

Any flying machine has to overcome air resistance: the friction caused when a solid moves through the air.
You can feel this on your skin and in your hair when you move quickly.

How to land an airship

I stood in the control room while the Captain told the crew how to land the ship.

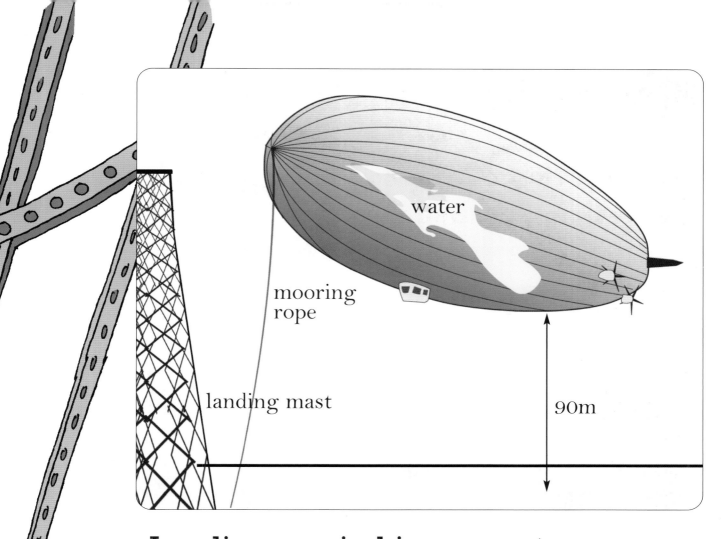

water

mooring
rope

landing mast

90m

Landing an airship was not easy:

1. Fly to the landing field at 200m (650ft).
2. Use the engines to slow down and help you face into the wind.
3. Release water ballast to keep the airship level.
4. At 90m (295ft) drop the mooring ropes.
5. Tie the airship to the landing mast.
6. Winch the airship down to the ground.

Disaster!

I heard a bang and shouts. When I looked behind me there were flames racing towards me. I ran, but found I was heading straight into the fire.

No-one knows what caused the fire on the *Hindenburg*. Some believe it was an accident, others that it was deliberate. But once a spark reached the hydrogen gas, the sky was lit with flames and the airship was completely ablaze in 37 seconds.

Live report

I saw people jump. Should I try that? Then someone appeared out of the smoke and dragged me away to safety.
I could smell perfume.

These are extracts from journalist Herbert Morrison's live radio report.

"" It's practically standing still now. They've dropped ropes out of the nose of the ship.

It's burst into flames!

It's falling and crashing!

Oh my, get out of the way!

I can't talk, ladies and gentlemen.

Honest, it's just lying there, a mass of smoking wreckage.

I can hardly breathe…

Listen folks, I'm gonna have to stop for a minute because I've lost my voice.

This is the worst thing I've ever witnessed. ""

Survived

I limped away from the wreckage, passing a radio reporter who was crying into his microphone.

There were 36 passengers and 61 crew on board. Of these, 13 passengers and 22 crew died, plus one worker on the ground. Most of the fatalities were people who jumped from the ship: nearly all who stayed aboard survived, although some were badly burned.

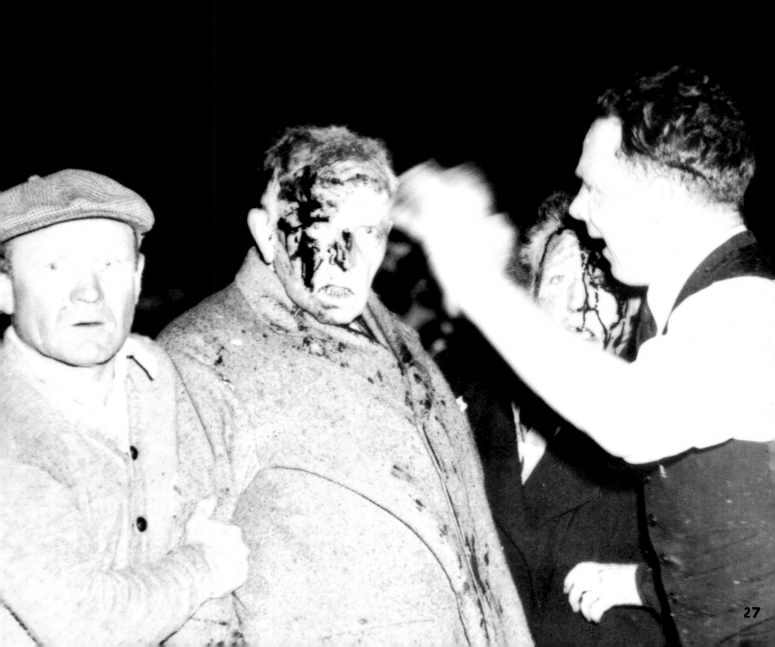

End of an era

I was too scared to fly home. They put me on a ship. When I got back my parents were furious. But Franz said it was our best dare yet!

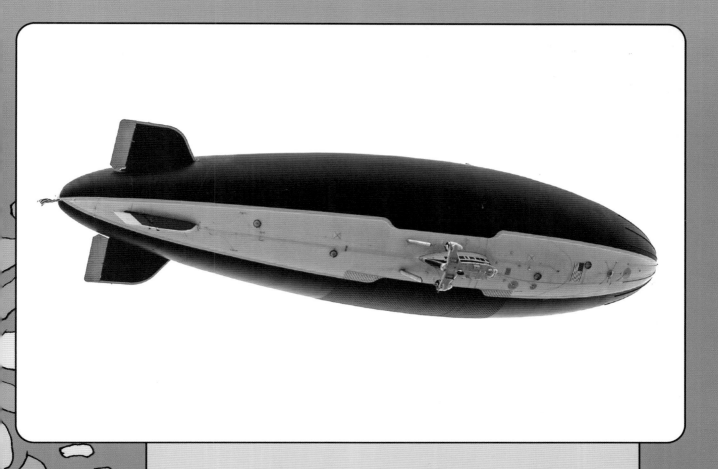

Although this was only the first major crash, people lost their faith in airship travel and went back to ships and planes.

Today, airships are used for advertising, sightseeing and research. It is possible that they will be used for cargo and passenger journeys again. Today's airships use helium.

Glossary

Ballast: heavy material used to keep a ship steady
Cell: part of a space that is divided off
Evaporate: when heat turns liquid to gas
Flammable: burns easily
Horsepower: the number of horses that would be needed to do the same work
Rigid: won't bend

Webography

http://history.howstuffworks.com/american-history/hindenburg.htm
This site has lots of background information on the Hindenburg disaster, such as how people travelled in the 1930s and how the Hindenburg was built.

http://www.vidicom-tv.com/tohiburg.htm
At this site you can watch a slideshow of Hindenburg images as well as a film of the disaster itself.

http://www.yourdiscovery.com/video/mythbusters-hindenburg-disaster/?cc=US
Watch what happened when investigators built a model of the Hindenburg to try to discover what caused the original airship to catch fire.

http://encyclopedia.kids.net.au/page/hi/Hindenburg_disaster
This website has plenty of facts and figures about the Hindenburg airship.

Index

If you enjoyed this book, look out for another Take 2 title:

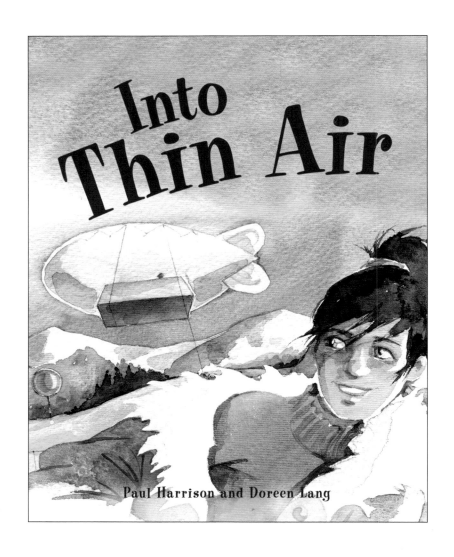

an adventure set in a weather research laboratory where Imogen follows clues to work out who is stealing secret data.